If you want a pretty maid,
Please choose me.

Jeremiah,
   blow the fire,
      Puff, puff, puff.

First you blow it gently

Quentin Blake's
NURSERY RHYME
BOOK

RED FOX

RED FOX
UK | USA | Canada | Ireland | Australia
India | New Zealand | South Africa

Red Fox is part of the Penguin Random House group of companies
whose addresses can be found at global.penguinrandomhouse.com.

www.penguin.co.uk   www.puffin.co.uk   www.ladybird.co.uk

The author and publishers are grateful to Oxford University Press for permission
to use the rhymes, some from Iona and Peter Opie's *Oxford Dictionary of
Nursery Rhymes* (1951) and some from their *Oxford Nursery Rhyme Book* (1955).

Penguin
Random House
UK

First published by Jonathan Cape 1983
Red Fox edition published 1995
This edition published 2018
001

Made and printed in China
A CIP catalogue record for this book is available from the British Library

ISBN: 978–1–782–95865–9

All correspondence to:
Red Fox, Penguin Random House Children's
80 Strand, London WC2R 0RL

MIX
Paper from
responsible sources
FSC
www.fsc.org
FSC® C018179

Little Jack Sprat
   Once had a pig,
It was not very little,
   Nor yet very big,
It was not very lean,
   It was not very fat –
It's a good pig to grunt,
   Said little Jack Sprat.

OINK

Ickle ockle, blue bockle,
Fishes in the sea,

Then you blow it rough.

Handy spandy, Jack-a-Dandy
Loves plum cake and sugar candy.
He bought some at a
grocer's shop

And out he came,
hop, hop,
hop, hop!

Gregory Griggs,
Gregory Griggs,
Had twenty-seven
different wigs.

He wore them up,
he wore them down
To please the people
of the town;

He wore them east,
   he wore them west,
But he never could tell
   which he loved the best.

Dickery, dickery, dare,
  The pig flew up in the air;

The man in brown
   soon brought him down,
Dickery, dickery, dare.

I had a little husband
　　No bigger than my thumb;
I put him in a pint pot
　　And there I bid him drum.
I gave him some garters
　　To garter up his hose,
And a little silk handkerchief
　　To wipe his pretty nose.

Pussy Cat ate the dumplings,
　　Pussy Cat ate the dumplings,
Mama stood by,
　　And cried, Oh, fie!
　　Why did you eat
　　　　the dumplings?

William McTrimbletoe,
  He's a good fisherman,

Catches fishes

Puts them in dishes,

Catches hens
    Puts them in pens,

Some lay eggs

Some lay none

William McTrimbletoe,
He doesn't eat one.

Pretty John Watts,
We are troubled with rats,
Will you drive them out of the house?

We have mice, too, in plenty
That feast in the pantry,
But let them stay,
And nibble away:
What harm is a little brown mouse?

Little Blue Ben,
who lives in the glen,
Keeps a blue cat
and one blue hen

Which lays of blue eggs
                a score and ten;
Where shall I find
                the little Blue Ben?

Goosey, goosey gander,
Who stands yonder?
Little Betsy Baker;

Take her up
and shake her.

Terence McDiddler,

The three-stringed fiddler,

Can charm, if you please,

The fish from the seas!

Robin the Bobbin
the big-bellied Ben
He ate more meat
than fourscore men.

He ate a cow
he ate a calf
He ate a butcher
and a half

He ate a church
    he ate a steeple
He ate a priest
    and all the people

A cow and a calf
A butcher and a half
A church and a steeple
And all the good people

And yet he complained
    That his stomach wasn't
            full.

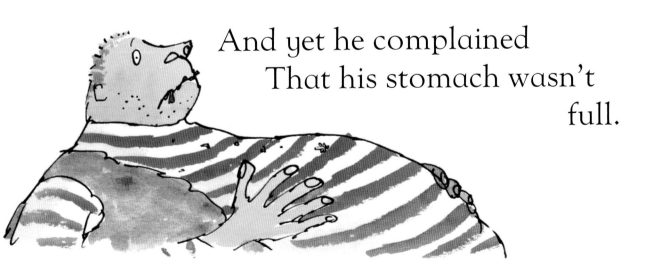

Here I am
Little Jumping Joan;

When nobody's with me
I'm all alone.

Oh, Mother,
I shall be married
 To Mr Punchinello,

To Mr Punch,
 To Mr Joe,
  To Mr Nell,
   To Mr Lo,

Mr Punch, Mr Joe,
Mr Nell, Mr Lo,
To Mr Punchinello!

Some other books by
Quentin Blake

All Join In
Angel Pavement
Angelica Sprocket's Pockets
Angelo
Clown
Cockatoos
Fantastic Daisy Artichoke
The Green Ship
Jack and Nancy
Loveykins
Mister Magnolia
Mrs Armitage and the Big Wave
Mrs Armitage on Wheels
Mrs Armitage Queen of the Road
Patrick
Quentin Blake's ABC
A Sailing Boat in the Sky
Snuff
Zagazoo